HARRY, THE HONEST HORSE

HARRY, THE HONEST HORSE

KA MULENGA

© Kalenga Augustine Mulenga 2021

Harry, The Honest Horse

Published by Kalenga Augustine Mulenga
augustine@kamulenga.com

ISBN 978-1-991202-00-0

2 4 6 8 10 9 7 5 3 1

Publication facilitation by Boutique Books

Printed in South Africa

This is dedicated to my wife, Sheba, and my three kids: Grace, Malaika, and Kalenga Jr. Thank you for believing in me.

Harry, The Honest Horse.

Harry was a young and handsome horse with a sleek black mane and a long swishy tail. He lived in Horseville, a lush meadow filled with green grass, pretty flowers and glassy lakes.

Because of his jolly nature, Harry had lots of friends in Horseville. They all loved to run around the meadow together, singing and having the time of their lives.

Harry's best friend was a horse called Hank. Hank loved horsing around and was always getting into trouble. He was also always telling fibs to get himself out of being punished.

"Why do you always tell lies when you get into trouble?" Harry would ask Hank.

"It's all just a game, Harry. It's all just for fun," Hank would reply. "How boring life would be if we were all honest! Now, come with me..."

Every day, Hank would come up with a new, naughty thing to do. Because Hank was his best friend, Harry would always follow him and do whatever he told him to do.

One morning, Hank came up with a plan to take all the hay from the old couple, Mr and Mrs Neigh, and hide it away from them. Harry and Hank trotted over to Mr and Mrs Neigh's eating trough in the middle of the night, took all their hay and hid it far, far away, down by the glassy lake.

When Mr and Mrs Neigh woke up the next morning, they went to the trough to eat their delicious hay breakfast. But there was nothing in the trough! Mr and Mrs Neigh asked Harry and Hank, "Did you see who took our hay?"

Before Harry could answer, Hank, who was very good at making up fibs, said, "There was a great wind last night and it swooped up all the hay from the trough!"

Mr and Mrs Neigh believed Hank's story and went to their neighbour's house to look for more hay to eat.

Hank was so happy that his fib had worked. But Harry was not happy with Hank. "You lied to that old couple and now they don't have any hay to eat!" he said to him, crossly.

"It's all just a game, Harry. It's all just for fun," Hank replied. "How boring life would be if we were all honest! Now, come with me..."

Harry felt he couldn't argue with Hank, because he was his best friend.

*B*ut when Harry came home that night, he went straight to his Dad.

"Dad, Hank is always telling lies and being dishonest. When I ask him why he does it he says, "It's all just a game, Harry. It's all just for fun. How boring life would be if we were all honest! Now, come with me..."

"Son," Harry's Dad replied, "Honesty is always the best policy, you'll see."

The next day, Hank and Harry met up as usual. Hank said to Harry, "I wonder what fun we can have today!"

They went back to Mr and Mrs Neigh's house. When they got there, Hank kicked over all the water from the drinking barrel. Off he trotted, laughing all the way.

But this time, Harry didn't trot after him.

When Mrs Neigh came out for a drink of water, she found that the drinking barrel was empty.

"Harry, what happened to all the water?" she asked.

Harry remembered what his dad had said and he decided to tell Mrs Neigh what Hank had done.

"Thank you for your honesty, Harry!" she said. "Here are four shiny red apples for you. You can come by every day for a treat!"

When Hank came looking for Harry, Harry told him what had happened. He said that he had decided to tell Mrs Neigh the truth, and that she had given him four shiny red apples to thank him for his honesty.

When Hank heard this news, he finally recognised his mistake.

"I guess it's not all just a game, Harry!" he said. "I guess it's not all just for fun. Life is not really boring when we are all honest – it's actually better for everyone!"

Also By K.A. Mulenga

Donk and The Stubborn Donkeys

Spike and Spud , The Spaceboys

Joe Finds His Way Home

The Leopard Licks Its Spots

Will and His Best Friend Whale

Polly the Polecat

Chuck the Cheetah

Imbwa, the Story of the Dog and His Harsh Master

Thank you for reading **Harry, The Honest Horse,** I hope you enjoyed it! Please let K.A. Mulenga know about what you thought about the book by leaving a short review on Amazon, it will help other parents and children find the story.(If you're under 13, ask a grown up to help you)

Top Tip: Be sure not to give away any of the story's secrets!

Sign up to my readers' club weekly newsletter.

Simply click on the YES, SIGN ME UP button on my website.

I will never share your email address. Unsubscribe at any time.

Printed in Great Britain
by Amazon